Thank you to my father, Demetrius, and my mother, Calnetra, for always believing in me and supporting me. Thank you to my family and friends, who traveled to watch me play since the age of four. Thank you to Georgia Elite Sports Academy for starting a program in Henry County that inspired me to develop a passion for football.

www.mascotbooks.com

All Through the Game

For more information, please contact:
Mascot Books, an imprint of Amplify Publishing Group
620 Herndon Parkway, Suite 320
Herndon, VA 20170
info@mascotbooks.com

Library of Congress Control Number: 2022901170

CPSIA Code: PRT0322A

ISBN-13: 978-1-63755-011-3

Printed in the United States

ALL THROUGH
the Game

DEMETRIUS PURVIS II

Illustrated by iNDOS Studio

THE TEAM ON THE FIELD SAID,

"GO TEAM GO!
GO TEAM GO!
GO TEAM GO!"

THE TEAM ON THE FIELD SAID,

"GO TEAM GO!"

ALL THROUGH THE GAME.

THE PLAYERS ON THE FIELD WERE

READY TO PLAY,
READY TO PLAY,
READY TO PLAY.

THE PLAYERS ON THE FIELD WERE

READY TO PLAY,

ALL THROUGH THE GAME.

THE CROWD IN THE STANDS SAID,

"SCORE, SCORE, SCORE!
SCORE, SCORE, SCORE!
SCORE, SCORE, SCORE!"

THE CROWD IN THE STANDS SAID,

"SCORE, SCORE, SCORE!"

ALL THROUGH THE GAME.

WHEN THE HELMETS HIT TOGETHER, THEY

CLACKED, CLACKED, CLACKED,
CLACKED, CLACKED, CLACKED,
CLACKED, CLACKED, CLACKED.

WHEN THE HELMETS HIT TOGETHER, THEY

CLACKED, CLACKED, CLACKED,

ALL THROUGH THE GAME.

THE COACH ON THE SIDE JUMPED

UP AND DOWN,
UP AND DOWN,
UP AND DOWN.

THE COACH ON THE SIDE JUMPED

UP AND DOWN,

ALL THROUGH THE GAME.

DTHEBEAST ON THE FIELD WENT

JUKE, JUKE, JUKE,
JUKE, JUKE, JUKE,
JUKE, JUKE, JUKE.

DTHEBEAST ON THE FIELD WENT

JUKE, JUKE, JUKE,

ALL THROUGH THE GAME.

THE REF IN THE GAME THREW

FLAGS, FLAGS, FLAGS,
FLAGS, FLAGS, FLAGS,
FLAGS, FLAGS, FLAGS.

THE REF IN THE GAME THREW

FLAGS, FLAGS, FLAGS,

ALL THROUGH THE GAME.

WHEN THE KICKER KICKED THE BALL, IT

FLIPPED, FLIPPED, FLIPPED,
FLIPPED, FLIPPED, FLIPPED,
FLIPPED, FLIPPED, FLIPPED.

WHEN THE KICKER KICKED THE BALL, IT

FLIPPED, FLIPPED, FLIPPED,

ALL THROUGH THE GAME.

THE BALL HIT THE POST AND

DINGED, DINGED, DINGED,
DINGED, DINGED, DINGED,
DINGED, DINGED, DINGED.

THE BALL HIT THE POST AND

DINGED, DINGED, DINGED,

ALL THROUGH THE GAME.

EVERYONE AT THE GAME YELLED,

"WIN, WIN, WIN!
WIN, WIN, WIN!
WIN, WIN, WIN."

EVERYONE AT THE GAME YELLED,

"WIN, WIN, WIN!"

ALL THROUGH THE GAME.

ABOUT the AUTHOR

Demetrius Purvis II was born in Charlotte, N.C. He is a skilled athlete, entrepreneur, and author. He plays football for Georgia Elite Sports Academy, better known as GESA. Demetrius also plays basketball and runs track for Henry County Parks & Rec. He was introduced to the game of football at the age of four. At age five, he scored five touchdowns in a single game and was given the name "DTHEBEAST." Football is Demetrius' favorite sport, and he trains four days a week and completes 200 push-ups every day. He is also the creator of a clothing line named DTHEBEAST APPAREL and the co-owner of K-FRESH AIR FRESHENER.